W9-CMI-799

Dear Parent:

Congratulations! Your child is taking the first steps on an exciting journey. The destination? Independent reading!

STEP INTO READING® will help your child get there. The program offers five steps to reading success. Each step includes fun stories and colorful art. There are also Step into Reading Sticker Books, Step into Reading Math Readers, Step into Reading Phonics Readers, Step into Reading Write-In Readers, and Step into Reading Phonics Boxed Sets—a complete literacy program with something for every child.

Learning to Read, Step by Step!

Ready to Read   Preschool–Kindergarten
• big type and easy words • rhyme and rhythm • picture clues
For children who know the alphabet and are eager to begin reading.

Reading with Help   Preschool–Grade 1
• basic vocabulary • short sentences • simple stories
For children who recognize familiar words and sound out new words with help.

Reading on Your Own   Grades 1–3
• engaging characters • easy-to-follow plots • popular topics
For children who are ready to read on their own.

Reading Paragraphs   Grades 2–3
• challenging vocabulary • short paragraphs • exciting stories
For newly independent readers who read simple sentences with confidence.

Ready for Chapters   Grades 2–4
• chapters • longer paragraphs • full-color art
For children who want to take the plunge into chapter books but still like colorful pictures.

STEP INTO READING® is designed to give every child a successful reading experience. The grade levels are only guides. Children can progress through the steps at their own speed, developing confidence in their reading, no matter what their grade.

Remember, a lifetime love of reading starts with a single step!

© 2004, 2014 Viacom International Inc. All rights reserved. Published in the United States
by Random House Children's Books, a division of Random House, Inc., 1745 Broadway,
New York, NY 10019, and in Canada by Random House of Canada Limited, Toronto.
Previously published in slightly different form by Simon Spotlight, a division of
Simon & Schuster, Inc., New York, in 2004. Nickelodeon, Dora the Explorer, and all related titles,
logos, and characters are trademarks of Viacom International Inc.

Step into Reading, Random House, and the Random House colophon are registered trademarks
of Random House, Inc.

Visit us on the Web!
StepIntoReading.com
randomhouse.com/kids

Educators and librarians, for a variety of teaching tools, visit us at RHTeachersLibrarians.com

ISBN 978-0-385-37459-0 (trade) — ISBN 978-0-385-37460-6 (lib. bdg.)
Printed in the United States of America

10 9 8 7 6 5 4 3 2 1

Random House Children's Books supports the First Ammendment and celebrates the right to read.

STEP INTO READING®

STEP 1

nickelodeon

DORA the EXPLORER™

I Love My Papi!

By Alison Inches

Illustrated by Dave Aikins

Random House 🏠 New York

Hi! I'm Dora.

I love to spend time with my <u>papi</u>.

Papi teaches me
a soccer kick.

I kick the ball.
Goal!

When we play baseball,
Papi coaches my team.

I swing the bat.

I slide into home!

On weekends,

Papi and I ride bikes.

Or we sail

on a boat.

In the summer,
we go
to the beach.

We build
sand castles.
We play
in the waves!

Papi is a good cook.

We bake a cake.

Yum! Yum!

15

Sometimes we pack
a picnic.
We share it
with Boots.

Papi can build
anything.

He makes us
a tire swing!

For a treat,
Papi takes us
to the circus.
Boots loves the clowns.

Every night,
Papi tucks me
into bed.

Then we read
a book.
I like books
about animals.

I love my <u>papi</u>!

And my <u>papi</u> loves me.